The Ups and Downs
of
Simpson Snail

by John Himmelman

PUFFIN BOOKS

To my son, Jeff—
may *your* ups greatly
outnumber your downs!

PUFFIN BOOKS
Published by the Penguin Group
Penguin Putnam Inc., 375 Hudson Street, New York, New York 10014, U.S.A.
Penguin Books Ltd, 27 Wrights Lane, London W8 5TZ, England
Penguin Books Australia Ltd, Ringwood, Victoria, Australia
Penguin Books Canada Ltd, 10 Alcorn Avenue, Toronto, Ontario, Canada M4V 3B2
Penguin Books (N.Z.) Ltd, 182-190 Wairau Road, Auckland 10, New Zealand

Penguin Books Ltd, Registered Offices: Harmondsworth, Middlesex, England

First published in the United States of America by E. P. Dutton, 1989
Published in a Puffin Easy-to-Read edition, 1997

3 5 7 9 10 8 6 4

THE LIBRARY OF CONGRESS HAS CATALOGED THE DUTTON EDITION AS FOLLOWS:
Himmelman, John.
The ups and downs of Simpson Snail/John Himmelman.—1st ed.
p. cm.
Summary: Four adventures of Simpson Snail as he visits a friend,
gets a new shell, tries to fly, and makes a statue.
ISBN 0-525-44542-0
[1. Snails—Fiction.] I. Title.
PZ7.H5686Up 1989 89-30547 [E]—dc19 CIP AC

Puffin Easy-to-Read ISBN 0-14-038726-9
Printed in the United States of America

Reading Level 1.7

Contents

Simpson Gets Stuck

Simpson woke up early.

"It is a nice morning,"

he said.

"I will visit my friend

Tucker Turtle.

We can have breakfast."

He put on his hiking hat.

And off he went.

Simpson came to the top

of a big hill.

Tucker lived at the bottom.

Almost there, thought Simpson.

It is a good thing, too.

I am very hungry.

He rushed

down the hill.

But Simpson slipped.

He began to roll down the hill.

Faster and faster he went.

Then he hit a bump.

Now Simpson was flying

down the hill!

He landed on a branch

and got stuck.

I will never get down from here,

he thought.

Just then Tucker walked under

Simpson's branch.

Simpson hoped

that Tucker

would not see him.

He felt very silly.

But Tucker did see him.

"What are you doing up there?"

Tucker asked.

"Oh, I am making believe

that I am a leaf."

"That sounds like fun,"

said Tucker.

"But why don't you come down?

We can have breakfast."

"Maybe later,"

said Simpson.

Tucker went back to his house.

Soon it was lunchtime.

Simpson was hungry.

Tucker came out to see him.

"Are you still a leaf?"

he asked.

Simpson still felt silly.

"No. Now I am a berry,"

he said.

A very hungry berry,

he thought.

"Will you come down

for lunch?"

asked Tucker.

"Maybe later,"

said Simpson.

Simpson sat there for a long time.

Then it was suppertime.

"Will you come down for supper?"

called the turtle.

"Or are you still a berry?"

"No, now I am resting,"

said Simpson.

"Being a berry is hard work."

It began to get dark.

Simpson did not want

to spend the night on the branch.

"Tucker! Tucker!" he called.

"I am stuck.

Please get me down!"

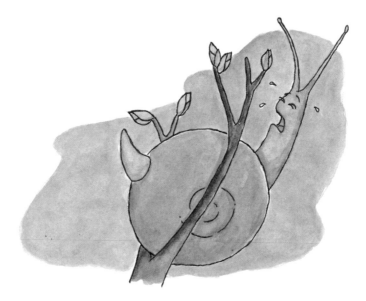

Tucker came out of his house.

He shook the branch.

Simpson fell to the ground.

"Come inside,"

said the turtle.

"I saved some breakfast

for a leaf.

I saved some lunch

for a berry.

And I saved supper

for a very tired snail."

And the tired snail

ate every bit of it!

A New Shell

Simpson looked in his mirror.

He frowned.

My shell is so old,

he thought.

I will look for a new one.

16

He looked under a big tree.

"What are you looking for?"

asked Graytail Squirrel.

"I need a new shell," said Simpson.

"This one is old and worn."

"I know just the thing," said Graytail.

He brought out

a big acorn shell.

Simpson slipped it on.

"It is nice for acorns," he said.

"But not for snails.

Thanks anyway."

Simpson saw Redwing Blackbird.

He was playing with his babies.

Simpson told him about his old shell.

"Lucky you," said Redwing.

"I have the perfect shell for you."

It was an eggshell.

Simpson tried it on.

"How do I look?" he asked.

"It looks better on a baby bird,"

said Redwing.

"Thanks anyway," said Simpson.

After a while, he met Carpenter Ant.

The ant was on his way to work.

"I will build you a new shell,"

he said.

"Could you?" asked Simpson.

The ant began right away.

Soon he had built Simpson

a brand-new shell!

"This one will look good on a snail.

Thank you,"

said Simpson.

"Don't mention it,"

said the ant.

Then he hurried off.

Simpson wanted to

show off the new shell.

He crawled inside it.

But he could not move.

It was too heavy.

Just then, Woolly Caterpillar

dropped onto Simpson's shell.

She crawled

up and down.

She crawled

back and forth.

Over and under

Simpson's shell

she crawled.

Then she jumped off.

Simpson looked at his old shell.

Woolly had cleaned and polished it

with her soft bristles.

Now it shone like new!

"Do you still want a new shell?"

asked Woolly.

"No, thank you," said Simpson.

"This one is perfect."

The Flight

Simpson and Tucker

loved to go to the beach.

So did their friend Gypsy Moth.

Gypsy loved the cool breeze.

Tucker loved the warm sun.

But Simpson loved the sea gulls.

"I wish I were a bird,"

said Simpson.

"But you are a snail.

That is good, too,"

said Gypsy.

It is not so great,

thought Simpson.

He watched the sea gulls.

One picked up a clam.

Up, up, up went the clam.

Way up into the sky.

Lucky clam,

thought Simpson.

But then the bird let go of the clam.

It crashed onto the rocks.

"Sea gulls open the shells that way,"

said Tucker.

"Then they eat the clams."

"Yuck,"

said Simpson.

But then he had an idea.

He crawled inside an empty clamshell.

"What are you doing?"

asked Gypsy.

"I am waiting for a sea gull,"

said the snail.

"He will carry me into the air."

"But he will drop you on the rocks,"

said Tucker.

"No, he won't," said Simpson.

"When I am high enough,

I will stick my head out.

The bird will see

that I am not a clam.

Then he will bring me down."

"You will get hurt," said Gypsy.

"Flying is not

for snails."

31

She was too late.

A sea gull grabbed Simpson.

Up, up, up he went.

Way up into the sky.

Simpson laughed.

He was flying like a bird!

Now it was time to come down.

He stuck his head out.

"I am not a clam,

Mr. Sea Gull,"

shouted Simpson.

Then the clamshell

broke in half!

Simpson fell.

"Help! Help!" he called.

Suddenly, Gypsy was under him.

But Simpson was too heavy.

She could not hold him.

They both fell into the water.

Tucker swam out to help them.

Gypsy climbed onto his back.

But Simpson's shell filled with water.

The snail started to sink.

He grabbed on to Tucker's tail.

The turtle pulled him out of the water.

"Being a flying snail

was not so bad,"

said Simpson.

"But I think I should

learn how to swim first."

Simpson's Statue

Simpson Snail looked

at his calendar.

"Today is Gypsy Moth's birthday,"

he said.

"I will make her something.

Something nice.

It will make her think of me."

Simpson went to Gypsy's house.

Gypsy was not home.

Simpson started to work.

He made a statue.

It looked just like Simpson!

Then Gypsy came home.

"Oh, Simpson!

This is the best present

in the world!" she said.

"When I look at it,

I will think of you."

Simpson was happy.

It felt good to give nice presents.

That night it rained.

In the morning,

everything was covered with mud.

Simpson went to see Gypsy.

"Will you play with me?"

he asked.

"I am sorry," said Gypsy.

"But my statue is muddy.

It will take me all day

to clean it."

"I understand,"

said Simpson.

The next morning,

Simpson went back to Gypsy's.

"Will you play today?"

he asked.

"I wish I could," said Gypsy.

"But I am planting flowers.

They will look nice

around my statue."

Simpson went home.

The next morning,

he was back at Gypsy's.

"Now do you have time to play?"

he asked.

"If only I did," said Gypsy.

"But I cannot see the statue

from my house.

So I am trimming

the weeds.

When I am done,

we can play."

"Maybe,"

said Simpson.

The snail went home.

He wished he had never made

that statue for Gypsy.

She likes it better

than she likes me, he thought.

Then he had an idea.

He made another statue.

This one looked like Gypsy.

"This Gypsy will have time for me,"

he said.

Simpson sat with his new friend.

But it wasn't the same.

This Gypsy was no fun.

Then the real Gypsy showed up.

"I am done with my work,"

she said.

"Would you like to play now?"

Simpson's feelings were still hurt.

"No," he said.

"I am playing

with my new friend."

"Can I join you?"

asked Gypsy.

"I miss my friend Simpson Snail."

"Do you miss

the *real* Simpson?"

asked the snail.

"I miss the *only* Simpson,"

said Gypsy.

And the real Gypsy

and the real Simpson

had a real good laugh.